★ My Dad's GTO ★

R. Curtis Roehm

AuthorHouse™
1663 Liberty Drive
Bloomington, IN 47403
www.authorhouse.com
Phone: 1-800-839-8640

First published by AuthorHouse 8/30/2011
ISBN: 978-1-4634-4379-5 (sc)
Library of Congress Control Number: 2011914150

Printed in the United States of America
This book is printed on acid-free paper.

authorHOUSE®

One spring day while I was in my backyard playing basketball, my dad came outside and said, "Son, how do you feel about taking a road trip tomorrow?" It sounded like fun, so I said, "Sure, where are we going?" He told me he had found a car that he wanted to buy in northern Indiana, which was about four hours away.

Later, during dinner that night, he told me that the car was a 1966 Pontiac GTO, but it would need a lot of work before we could drive it. As I helped myself to a second helping of macaroni and cheese, he told me he thought it would be the perfect project for us to work on together. "You are going to have to go to bed early tonight because we have to get up very early," he said.

That night, after I said my prayers, I was lying there thinking about all of the fun we were going to have. It seemed like as soon as I closed my eyes, he was in my room, waking me up and telling me it was time to leave. It was so early it was still dark outside! It was only six o'clock in the morning, but I rolled out of bed, put on my clothes, and climbed into the truck.

Before we got on the freeway, we made a quick stop for breakfast. I was hungry, and my dad needed a big cup of coffee for the trip. Once we were on the road, my dad reached into the console, pulled out a CD, and said, "I made a special CD for us to listen to today. It is packed full of old car songs." I rolled my window down so I could feel the cool breeze against my face and started singing the ones I knew. I was shocked when I heard songs about GTOs. My favorite song was "Little GTO." It made me tap my feet and clap my hands. While we were listening, I started asking my dad questions about the car. I knew I could ask him anything because he had owned ten GTOs. He was a genius when it came to cars. I learned that the GTO marked the beginning of the muscle car era, that the first GTO was made in 1964, and that GTO stood for *Gran Turismo Omologato.* I wasn't sure what that meant, but it sure sounded cool.

The trip went fast, and we were there before I knew it. The owner walked out of his house and met us in the driveway with a smile and a handshake. He led us to the field where the car was sitting. It had been broken down there for twenty years. It looked a little rusty to me. The paint was faded, the tires were flat, the seats were ripped, and it didn't even have an engine. But my dad said he could see the true beauty underneath all of that. I took his word for it.

When it was time to load the car on the trailer, we had to use a special tool called a winch. It pulled the car onto the trailer for us, so we didn't have to push. I helped to make sure all of the straps were tight, so the car wouldn't fall off on the trip home.

After we put the car on the trailer, we were ready to start back home. We gave the man his money, shook his hand again, and got into the truck. As we drove away, the man shouted, "Be sure to send me pictures when you are finished restoring her." On the way home we talked about what kind of work we would have to do to get the car ready for the road.

My dad told me that his father, my grandpa, also enjoyed working on cars. He taught him how to work on them when he was about my age. I learned that a long time ago, my grandpa owned a service station. At that time it was the biggest one in our hometown, and the only one that could work on more than one car at a time. Then we had to stop talking because I was getting tired from all of the excitement; I decided it was time to take a nap.

I woke up as we were pulling into our neighborhood. My mom heard us pull up to the house and came outside to see our car. She started laughing and called it a rust bucket. She doubted that we would ever finish it, but we didn't care. We knew we could fix the GTO.

There was a lot of hard work to be done, and I wanted to be in the garage working next to my dad every second I could. I would come straight home from school, sit at the kitchen table, and do my homework. When I finished, I would have my mom check it to make sure it was right. After she gave me permission, I would blast out the door to see what was happening in the garage.

My dad always had plenty of work for me to do. Sometimes I would use sandpaper and help sand away old paint and rust. Other times I would use a ratchet to remove pieces of the car that had to be replaced. My favorite thing to do was sit and watch my dad work. He taught me how to use some pretty cool tools. I really liked wearing the big mask and watching him use the welder to fix holes in the car. The masks were so dark we couldn't see anything until he started welding. As we worked, my dad would remind me that one day, when I was older and had a driver's license, I would get to drive this beautiful goat. Goat is a nickname for the GTO. I think it is a funny name, but a lot of people still call them that.

Knowing I would be driving this car made me want work extra hard and do my best job. After we finished fixing the rust and holes, it was time to paint the car. My dad decided to paint it gold because that is the color it had been when it was new. It looked awesome with a fresh coat of paint. Once the car was painted, it was time to start working on the engine. Since there wasn't one in the car, my dad used one he had in the garage. He had tons of extra car parts. He left me in charge of cleaning and scraping all of the old dirt and oil off the engine. After many hours of washing, wiping, and drying, we painted the engine. Pontiac engines were blue in the sixties, so that's the color we used to make it look new. After we painted the engine, my dad started to put all of the pieces back together. My dad showed me a special tool called a torque wrench. He said it was important to use one every time you worked on an engine, but he also told me I would have to wait a few more years before I could use it.

When he finished putting it all together, it was time to put the engine in the car for the first time. It was so heavy that we used a big tool called an engine hoist. I was in charge of raising and lowering the engine while my dad pushed, pulled, and tugged on the engine until it was sitting in the perfect spot. When I heard it start for the first time, it gave me chills. It was very loud and rumbled like a racecar.

It took a long time to get the GTO ready for the road, but after many weeks of hard work, we were ready to take her for a spin. We pulled the car out of the garage and honked the horn. My mom came outside and looked very surprised. She thought the car was perfect. She walked up to my side of the car, leaned in through the window, and looked at me sitting in the passenger's seat. She said, "You and your father make a great team!" I smiled, thinking about what she said.

The GTO looked so good that we decided to take it to a car show. There were more than one hundred cars competing against each other. Many people stopped to look at our car and said we had done a great job. We had the only GTO at the show. I was snacking on a Twizzler when a man with a microphone started talking. The man said, "It is now time to announce the winner of the best of show award. This year, the award goes to ... the 1966 GTO." I dropped my Twizzler and started jumping up and down. Everyone was cheering for us as we walked up to receive our award.

The trophy we won was taller than I was, even when I stood on my tippy toes. It felt great to be standing on the stage with my hero, my dad. As people were taking our pictures, I smiled as I thought about all of the fun we'd had together. While we slowly walked off the stage and headed to our car to leave, I looked up at my dad and said, "I love you, Dad."

CPSIA information can be obtained
at www.ICGtesting.com
Printed in the USA
247067LV00002B

9 781463 443795